NORA'S STARS

Satomi Ichikawa

Philomel Books · *New York*

One summer Nora and her dog Kiki, her doll Maggie, and Teddy the stuffed bear came to visit Nora's grandmother, who lived in a place where the sun seemed always to be shining and where the scent of sweet fruits and green trees was always in the air. Even grandmother's house was the color of the sun.

"Look, Kiki," Nora said as she unlatched the gate. "Grandmother's house nearly touches the sky."

"We're here," she called to her grandmother as she and Kiki ran up the long stairs.

There was much to discover. "See, these hibiscus flowers,"
Grandmother said to Nora. "They open when the sun rises and
close with the sunset. My turtle is always awake to see the flowers
open." Grandmother smiled. "If you want to see them open, you
will have to get up early, too." Kiki was satisfied just to see the turtle.

Nora loved plums.

"If you want plums, just shake the tree," Grandmother told her. She shook the plum tree, and plums fell all around Nora. Maggie and Teddy pretended they didn't notice.

That night Nora went to bed early.
In the morning she and her friends
would have plum jam near the
hibiscus flower. Perhaps they would
see the turtle. "Good night,
Grandmother," she called.

Nora had just climbed into a bed with Maggie and Teddy when she heard a strange noise. Kiki heard it too.

But Grandmother was downstairs. Who was making the noise in the room?

Nora sat up. In the corner there was a trunk full of toys
that had been in Grandmother's house a long time. Now
the toys were beginning to jump out of the trunk. "Oh!"
said Nora. Maggie and Teddy could not believe their eyes.
"Will you play with me?" Nora asked the toys.

"Let's play outside. It's hot inside," a brown bear said. It opened the door, and the toy dolls and animals ran out to the balcony. Nora and her friends did too.

"Look at the stars," she said. "They look so pretty and they are so close. I would love to have those stars."

"But that is easy," said a dancing doll, and all the toys flew up into the sky to get the stars for Nora.

When they had gathered all of the stars in the sky, the toys decorated the bedcover for her. "Now you are Princess Nora," a clown said to her. "A star princess." Kiki nearly got lost in her cape.

Suddenly there was a knock at the door. Nora quickly put the stars into the trunk and climbed into bed. "Don't move," she whispered to the toys.

Grandmother opened the door and peeked around the corner, but Nora was quietly reading her book. Grandmother smiled and shut the door.

After Grandmother left, Nora threw open the lid
of the chest and let the stars out. She made a
necklace of stars and a crown of stars. She and her
toy friends made a train of stars. Nora gathered the
stars, rolled in them, danced with them. Stars
filled the room.

Then the door blew open. Nora
wondered why, and went outside to
see. Kiki went too. "Oh," she said.
"The sky is so dark now."

She felt a drop of water. "Is the sky crying?" she wondered.

She looked up. The sky looked sad without any stars. Inside her room the toys and Maggie and Teddy were still playing with all the stars in the world. They were having a wonderful time, but Nora was worried.

She decided to give the stars back. She gathered them all up in her bedcover and shook them, still twinkling, back into the sky.

Then Nora, Teddy, and Maggie went inside and climbed into bed.

The toys climbed back into the trunk.

Before many minutes had passed, Grandmother's house was sleeping, the trees and the flowers were sleeping, all the world was sleeping under Nora's stars. Nora yawned. "That's the way it should be," she murmured, and, satisfied, Nora went to sleep too.

For the Palmer family and all the children
who have spent their holidays in this house

The wonderful dolls that Nora discovered in her grandmother's trunk are
all based on real-life dolls from the collection of Satomi Ichikawa.

American text copyright © 1989 by Philomel Books.
Text and illustrations copyright © 1988 by Satomi Ichikawa.
All rights reserved.
Published in the United States by Philomel Books,
a division of The Putnam & Grosset Group,
200 Madison Avenue, New York, NY 10016.
Published simultaneously in Canada.
Originally published in 1988 in Japanese, under the title
Ohoshisama no Irutokoro, by Kaisei-Sha Publishing Co., Ltd., Tokyo.
English translation rights arranged with Kaisei-Sha Publishing Co., Ltd.,
through Japan Foreign-Rights Centre.
Printed in Hong Kong by South China Printing Co. (1988) Ltd.
Design by Christy Hale.

Library of Congress Cataloging-in-Publication Data: Ichikawa, Satomi. Nora's stars / by Satomi
Ichikawa. p. cm. Translated from the Japanese. Summary: While visiting her grandmother, Nora
joins with the animated toys from an old chest to bring the stars down from the night sky, but their
loss makes the sky black and sad. ISBN 0-399-21616-2   [1. Stars—Fiction.   2. Toys—Fiction.   3.
Sky—Fiction. 4. Grandmothers—Fiction.] I. Title. PZ7.I16Nu 1988 [E]   dc1988-9936 CIP AC
Second impression.